Other Wibbly Pig books:
Wibbly Pig likes bananas
Wibbly Pig can dance
Wibbly Pig is happy
Wibbly Pig makes pictures
Wibbly Pig opens his presents
Wibbly Pig makes a tent
The Wibbly Pig Collection
Everyone Hide from Wibbly Pig
In Wibbly's Garden

First published in 2004
by Hodder Children's Books,
a division of Hodder Headline Limited,
338 Euston Road, London NW1 3BH

Copyright © 2004 Mick Inkpen

The right of Mick Inkpen to be identified as
the author of this Work has been
asserted by him in accordance with the
Copyright, Designs and Patents Act 1988.

ISBN 0340 878630

2 4 6 8 10 9 7 5 3 1

A CIP catalogue record for this book
is available from the British Library.

Printed in China

Is it bedtime Wibbly Pig?

Mick Inkpen

Hodder
Children's
Books

A division of Hodder Headline Limited

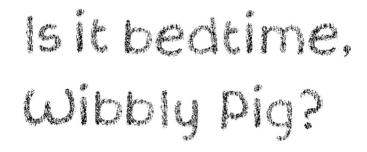

Is it bedtime,
Wibbly Pig?

No, silly!
I'm still in
the bath!

Have you finished
your bath, Wibbly Pig?

No.
I'm still drying
my toes.

Will you be long,
Wibbly Pig?

No, not long.

Are you ready for
bed now, Wibbly Pig?

No.
I'm finishing my story.

Have you finished
your drink, Wibbly Pig?

No, it's too hot,
isn't it Pigley?

Are you brushing your teeth, Wibbly Pig?

No.
I'm drawing
a picture
of Pigley.

Are you going up
to bed, Wibbly Pig?

No.
I'm counting
the stairs.

Aren't you sleepy,
Wibbly Pig?

No, I'm bouncy!

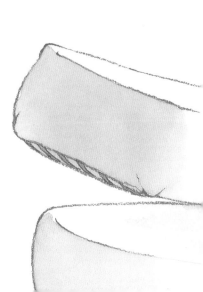

Shall we close the curtains, Wibbly Pig?

No.
I want to look
at the moon.

Do you want

Pigley,

or Flop,

or Dimple?

I want all of them.

Shall we turn out
the light, Wibbly Pig?

Wibbly Pig?

Wibbly Pig?

Are you asleep, Wibbly?

No, I'm dreaming!